RUDY

AND THE

MONSTER AT SCHOOL

OXFORD
UNIVERSITY PRESS

Great Clarendon Street, Oxford OX2 6DP
Oxford University Press is a department of the University of Oxford.
It furthers the University's objective of excellence in research, scholarship,
and education by publishing worldwide. Oxford is a registered trade mark
of Oxford University Press in the UK and in certain other countries

British Library Cataloguing in Publication Data

Data available

ISBN: 978-0-19-278251-9

1 3 5 7 9 10 8 6 4 2

Printed in Great Britain by Bell and Bain Ltd, Glasgow

Paper used in the production of this book is a natural,
recyclable product made from wood grown in sustainable forests.
The manufacturing process conforms to the environmental
regulations of the country of origin.

MIX
Paper from
responsible sources
FSC® C007785

RUDY
AND THE
MONSTER AT SCHOOL

WRITTEN BY
PAUL WESTMORELAND

PICTURES BY
GEORGE ERMOS

OXFORD
UNIVERSITY PRESS

ST RIGAMORE'S
ACADEMY

THE SKATEWAY

RUDY
WEREWOLF

🐾 Lives with:
Mum and Dad

🐾 Likes: skateboarding,
pizza, adventure!

🐾 Dislikes: baths

🐾 Personality: brave,
impulsive, mischievous,
kind

🐾 Best skateboard move:
The Daring Double!

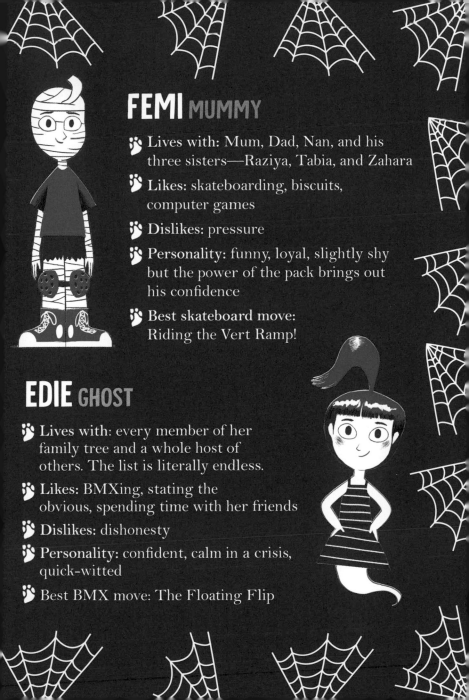

FEMI MUMMY

- 🐾 Lives with: Mum, Dad, Nan, and his three sisters—Raziya, Tabia, and Zahara
- 🐾 Likes: skateboarding, biscuits, computer games
- 🐾 Dislikes: pressure
- 🐾 Personality: funny, loyal, slightly shy but the power of the pack brings out his confidence
- 🐾 Best skateboard move: Riding the Vert Ramp!

EDIE GHOST

- 🐾 Lives with: every member of her family tree and a whole host of others. The list is literally endless.
- 🐾 Likes: BMXing, stating the obvious, spending time with her friends
- 🐾 Dislikes: dishonesty
- 🐾 Personality: confident, calm in a crisis, quick-witted
- 🐾 Best BMX move: The Floating Flip

CHAPTER
ONE

'It's a place where, they say, the lightning never stops flashing.' Edie's ghostly eyes glowed as she spoke. 'And the thunder is so loud it shakes your brain out of your ears!'

Femi was quaking in his bandages.

'High Crag Castle doesn't scare me,' Rudy said, rocking back on his chair. He let go of his desk and stretched out his wolf claws to keep his balance.

His friends stared at him.

'R-r-really?' Femi stammered. 'I'm glad that creepy castle is on the other side of Cobble Cross!'

'They also say monsters roam the

corridors,' Edie whispered. 'And it's haunted!'

'Err, everywhere you go is haunted,' Rudy replied, and the ghost girl rolled her eyes. 'We should go there tonight, after school. See if it's true.'

'Are you kidding?' Edie stared at him. 'We might never come back!'

'I wouldn't go even if you promised me one of these!' Femi said and held up a review of the new Pitbull-360 skateboard. 'Besides, I have to hit the Skateway tonight. I want to try out a Ramp Slam.'

'Wow! They'll be supreme!' Edie said.

Before Rudy could persuade them, a
flurry of black smoke rushed into the room
and the door shut with a . . .

SLAMMMM!

The smoke whipped up in a
tornado with a stomach-sickening
hissss and whirled into the form
of a wizened and dusty old
vampire.

'Good-morning-Mr-
Hunter,' said the class in
a monotone chorus.
No one was quite sure why
they did this; they just
felt oddly compelled to.

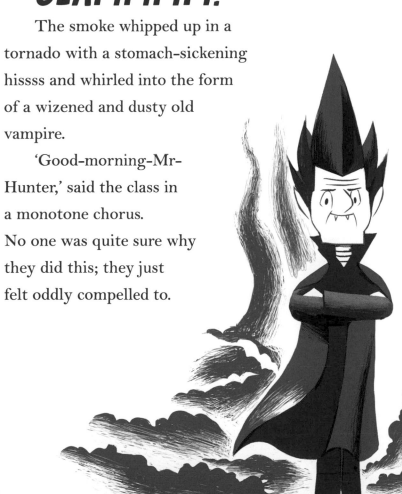

'Good morning, everybody,' the vampire replied with a lick of his fangs. 'I have some wonderful news.'

Mr Hunter snapped his fingers and the class fell silent. Even the banshee sisters, Wailer and Screech, and Jimmy Voll, the mouthy devilish captain of the school football team, listened intently.

Mr Hunter smiled. 'We have a new boy starting today. I suggest you make him feel very welcome.'

With a flick of his hand, the door flew open, and there stood a huge, imposing boy with heavy skater chains hanging off the belt of his baggy jeans. His muscles were bursting through the tears in his faded skull T-shirt while his beefy arms dangled out from the sleeves of his chequered shirt, almost touching the floor.

He wasn't just big and tall for his age, he was a clear head and shoulders above the entire class!

Rudy blinked in surprise as the whole class gawped at the monstrous new boy.

With an awkward, twisting shove of his shoulders and the sound of splintering wood, he muscled into the room. It was like a teddy bear visiting a doll's house!

First came his flat-top—not the hairstyle, the top of his head was actually

flat! His hair was blackened and singed and sprouted out in awkward clumps. And across his forehead was a deep train-track scar.

The huge boy looked at the class with two drooping eyes that had bags like he hadn't slept in years. He swallowed, drawing everyone's eyes to the tightened bolts in his neck, and made a grimacing smile.

No one knew what to say. They hadn't seen anyone like this before.

'Frankie, welcome to our school. Won't you please sit down?' Mr Hunter smiled and pointed a long, bony finger at an empty place on the table with Rudy, Femi, and Edie.

Frankie needed a seat, but he was big enough to fill two.

As he stepped over, one of Frankie's hulking metal boots caught on Femi's bandages. In one step, it wound around Frankie's ankles, pulled tight, and he toppled over like a felled tree . . .

BANG-
DRANNNNG!

He crashed onto the table, snapping all
four legs and karate-chopping the top in two.
Rudy pulled his legs out just in time. And
it was lucky Edie was already a ghost!

Before the splinters could settle, Wailer and Screech started screaming. And Jimmy Voll burst out laughing like it was the funniest thing he'd seen since Femi tried out for the school football team. The rest of the class saw this as a green light to join in.

'Suuuuusssssssssssssssssssh!' Mr Hunter hissed across the room. Everyone fell silent . . . and strangely sleepy.

Frankie sat up. His face didn't work very well, but Rudy could see how embarrassed he was.

'Sorry,' Frankie said. He spoke slowly, as though he thought about each word in turn. 'That stuff always happens to me.'

'Me too,' Femi replied as he untangled his bandages from Frankie's boots.

As Frankie found a chair, Mr Hunter sighed. 'Mr Abomasquash can't fix the table now. So please work on your knees.'

'It's OK, sir,' Rudy said as an idea jumped into his head. He set his skateboard across his lap. 'We can lean on these!'

Frankie's thighs were as big as tree trunks, so he just used them.

'Very good.' Mr Hunter smiled. 'Now everybody, please open your maths books and start working out the sums.'

Soon numbers and division, multiplication and minuses were filling Rudy's head. But he began to feel like he was the only person who was working.

Rudy looked up to see what was going on. Everyone around him kept checking Mr Hunter wasn't watching before stealing glances at Frankie. And Jimmy Voll was staring at him.

Rudy frowned.

He turned and looked at Frankie to see what everyone else was staring at.

But Frankie wasn't doing anything besides his maths. He was good at it, too, and was getting through the sums faster than Rudy!

Suddenly, Rudy felt a ghostly breath rush past his ear. 'Don't be mean,' Edie whispered.

'I wasn't!' Rudy replied.

'It's rude to stare,' she said.

Rudy realized Edie was right—as always! Rudy got back to work, but his brain was buzzing about Frankie. He was a conundrum.

An oversized, awkward misfit who spoke slowly. But he wasn't stupid. One look at his maths book said that much!

But the rest of the class couldn't see that. Certainly not from where Jimmy Voll was sitting!

People must stare at Frankie all the time, Rudy thought and began to feel bad for him.

Unfortunately, there was nothing Rudy could do about it now. His sums wouldn't do themselves . . .

Before Rudy knew it, his tummy was rumbling, and the lunchtime bell was ringing.

CHAPTER TWO

'Rudy, Femi, and Edie were first to arrive at the dining hall. Rudy's tummy rumbled like thunder as they took their lunch trays to their usual table by the window.

As they sat down, Frankie arrived with the rest of the class following him, like cars stuck behind a hay truck.

Frankie didn't think much of the lunch. Or rather, he didn't think there was very much of it.

'Everyone gets the same,' barked Ms Gunther, the dinner lady.

Rudy always appreciated the school dinners. The cook was a troll, and he'd seen what trolls eat!

As Frankie sat down, Jimmy Voll whispered: 'Be careful around Frankie. If he doesn't eat enough lunch, he might eat you!'

Everyone around him tried to hide their sniggers, but they were rubbish at it. They also didn't realize that thanks to his wolf-hearing, Rudy had heard everything. And he didn't like it one bit!

He was about to tell Edie and Femi when Screech whispered something else: 'I wouldn't go anywhere near Frankie. He could snap your arm like a toothpick, and he probably wouldn't notice!'

'I bet he only came here because his last school kicked him out,' mumbled Wailer. 'I mean, who'd want him smashing everything up?'

This is horrible! Rudy thought. He looked over at Frankie. He was sitting with his back to everyone, so Rudy couldn't tell if he'd heard them or not.

Suddenly Frankie pushed his chair back with a long, scraping—

EEEEKKKK- EEERRRRRRRRR!

The entire hall froze, terrified of what he might do.

But all Frankie did was get up, put his empty tray on the table by the door, and go out to the playground.

While the room filled with guilty giggles, Rudy was left feeling so sorry for Frankie he lost his appetite.

'Saying things like that is ridiculous,' Edie said as they strolled across the playground.

Femi nodded. 'I can't believe he goes around breaking arms and eating people when he hasn't had enough lunch.'

'Yeah, being clumsy doesn't make you a monster,' Rudy said as a football shot towards them.

Rudy stopped it and went to kick it back.

'Wanna play?' Jimmy Voll asked.

'Do you need a referee?' Edie asked, pulling a whistle from her pocket.

'We need all the help we can get!' Jimmy replied.

Rudy wanted to join in, but losing always put Jimmy in a vile mood. As he weighed it up, Femi gave him a nudge. Frankie was already playing, so maybe Jimmy was playing nicely?

As soon as Edie blew the whistle, Rudy realized that Jimmy wasn't playing nicely at all. Whenever he or his friends got the ball, they'd scream and run away from Frankie and pass to anyone except him. Edie got frustrated with them too, but she couldn't give them yellow cards for that.

So Frankie spent the whole game standing in the middle of the pitch, struggling to keep up, and he was too slow to shout out for a pass.

As soon as Rudy got the ball, he turned
to Frankie and set up a pass. But as Frankie
turned round, Femi shouted, 'Over here!'

Femi was in the perfect position to
score and win the game. So Rudy turned and
passed the ball to his friend.

It flew past Frankie and Femi drew back
his foot to whack it into the net.

At least, that was the plan . . .

Femi's foot swung and—BANG!

He hoofed the ball into the air. It blasted

DUNK! DUNK!
DU-DUNK!

It landed on the tin roof of the
caretaker's shed and rolled into the guttering.

'Nice one, losers!' Jimmy yelled, and
everyone groaned at Rudy and Femi. 'You've
ruined the game. You and that giant disaster!'

Rudy and Femi felt terrible. But Frankie
just shrugged and scratched his head.

'Oh, ignore them,' Edie said as Rudy
burned with embarrassment. 'Jimmy's just
annoyed because his precious team is on a
major losing streak.'

Rudy smiled. His friends always made him feel better.

'I'm soooo sorry,' Femi said as they wandered over to the shed.

'It's OK. We can still help Jimmy win,' Rudy said.

'I wouldn't bank on it. The ball's properly stuck up there,' Edie said as she floated up to look on the roof. 'I'd get it but, you know.' She shrugged.

'Thanks.' Rudy smiled. He jumped up to dislodge the ball. It was one of his biggest jumps, but he was still nowhere close.

'Do you want to try a lasso?' Femi asked, unravelling one of his bandages.

'It's OK,' Rudy replied. 'What we need is a bench!'

Dragging a bench across the playground took longer than Rudy expected. It would've been quicker to borrow a ladder from Mr Abomasquash, but the caretaker was busy fixing the table Frankie broke in maths, and Rudy couldn't speak yeti.

As Rudy climbed on the bench and reached up to get the ball off the moss-pocked roof, the bell rang for afternoon lessons.

Rudy's heart sank to the ground. They'd used up the rest of break, and Jimmy Voll had lost the game—he'd never forgive them for this!

As Rudy climbed down, he saw Frankie trudging back to class. He looked so deflated his hands were scraping the ground. It was hardly surprising, and Rudy felt even worse. Frankie had done nothing wrong, but everyone was being so mean to him.But what could Rudy do?

Thoughts churned in Rudy's head, and suddenly he realized he should've asked Frankie to help get the ball back!

He's so big, and his arms are so long, he could've reached the ball in a second, and Jimmy Voll and everyone else could've played until the bell rang. They might've won!

Rudy jumped off the bench and headed to class with a firm decision made in his mind. He was going to try and get to know Frankie. Who knows, this clumsy great lump might not be a total monster?

CHAPTER
THREE

'Ah, Rudy. I am so pleased you could join my little science class.' Mr Hunter's hypnotic voice hissed as Rudy arrived slightly late.

Rudy opened his mouth to explain, but Mr Hunter's eyes turned dark and thundery. Rudy froze.

'Just. Sit. Down,' the old vampire said, and Rudy nodded.

'Now, for today's experiment, I would like you all to work in pairs,' Mr Hunter explained.

As Rudy looked around, the class shuffled their stools together. The Banshee sisters were always paired up, and Edie and Femi were sitting together, so Rudy couldn't join them.

The only person left was Frankie. Even though he took up most of his bench, this was the perfect chance for Rudy to get to know him.

To the surprise of Jimmy Voll and Frankie, Rudy happily sat next to the new boy and squeezed his books into the sliver of empty space.

As everyone set up their experiments, Rudy discovered that Frankie was really good with the equipment. He knew his conical flask from his beaker and could position a clamp stand over the Bunsen burner in seconds. He poured out the exact amount of water, weighed the crystals, and they started dissolving in no time!

'How do you know all this?' Rudy asked.

'My dad showed me. He has a lab,' Frankie replied.

'Wow! My dad only showed me how to work the TV remote.'

Frankie laughed. 'We don't have a TV any more. It exploded.'

'How?' Rudy gasped.

'We had a power surge. Dad was over the moon. He loves electricity. That's why we moved here. Our new place has loads of lightning. It never stops striking the roof.'

Rudy thought for a moment. Only one place in Cobble Cross had that much lightning . . .

The blood drained from Rudy's face as he realized Frankie

must have moved into High Crag Castle!

Was he one of the monsters that Edie said roamed the corridors?

Suddenly, Rudy's thoughts turned to nightmares. The last thing he wanted to do was upset a monster, so he quickly changed the subject. 'What about your friends?' He smiled. 'Will they visit you?'

Frankie shook his head, and the bolts in his neck let out a squeal. The sound sent a shiver through Rudy.

'It's too far,' Frankie said. 'Which is a shame; we used to love sitting in my old bell tower with Rocko, watching the lightning strike the conductors. It got pretty lively. Once it fried a passing crow!'

'Yikes,' Rudy thought but kept smiling. He liked to think he was fearless, but this was too much!

Rudy distracted himself by checking

the experiment. Everything was bubbling nicely—they might even impress Mr Hunter!

But before Rudy's thoughts could run away with him, a crystal hit the back of his ear. He turned round and caught Jimmy Voll sniggering with Trevor Dactil, the pointy-faced lizard boy.

Rudy tried to ignore them, but a minute later they did it again.

Rudy looked around, his blood boiling, and to his annoyance saw that everyone else was flicking crystals at Frankie.

Luckily, Frankie was too big to notice, but Rudy felt torn. He didn't want to tell everyone that Frankie was a monster from a scary old castle because that would make him as mean as they were. But he just wanted them to stop throwing . . .

'Argh!' Rudy exclaimed as another bit of crystal pinged against his neck and everyone started sniggering.

That's it!

Rudy turned and squirted a pipette of water at Jimmy and Trevor.

'Hey!' Jimmy cried as it splattered across his book, blurring his spidery notes.

The class gasped. Mr Hunter looked up. Frankie turned round and . . .

KER-RAASSSSSHHH!

Frankie and Rudy's entire apparatus toppled onto the floor. Metal stands and glass shards scattered everywhere in a shower of boiling water and undissolved crystals.

'WHAT IS GOING ON?!' Mr Hunter boomed, silencing everyone.

Rudy stared at his teacher. This wasn't his fault, but he didn't want everyone to think he was telling tales.

Frankie kept quiet too.

'No more messing about,' Mr Hunter said, gliding across the room. 'I want a full write-up of your experiment, first thing in the morning.'

Rudy's face fell. Extra homework only meant one thing—no time at the Skateway!

He glanced at Femi and Edie. They looked as disappointed as he was.

All he'd wanted to do was get to know Frankie, but hanging out with him had become a load of trouble Rudy could happily do without.

'Now clean up this mess!' Mr Hunter hissed.

Rudy nodded and went to get some paper tissues.

Then something went **K-SNAP!**
And Frankie said, 'Whoops.'

Rudy couldn't believe it. The clumsy oaf
had trodden on his skateboard. As Frankie
lifted up his heavy metal boot, Rudy saw it
was broken in two!

'My board!' Rudy cried in utter disbelief.

Now, not only was he missing out on tonight's visit to the Skateway and Femi's attempt at a Ramp Slam, thanks to Frankie, he wouldn't be going until he saved up for a new skateboard!

This was too much.

'ARGH!' Rudy yelled as his temper exploded. He didn't care how big Frankie was, how scary his house was, or what their hissy old vampire teacher might say; he was furious.

Frankie stared at him, looking as if his brain had short-circuited. Then it rebooted and he ran out of the lab.

Rudy was left standing there, seething with anger.

'Rudy,' Mr Hunter said. His voice was calm but felt as strong as steel. 'You'd better go outside and cool off.'

The old vampire waved his hand, and Rudy did as he was told.

Rudy sat by the lockers, alone in the corridor, with everything that had annoyed him and everything he'd shouted at Frankie stewing in his head. His lungs sucked in one deep breath after another, and gradually his anger slipped away like the tide.

But it left him feeling awful, like he was sick but not actually ill.

His skateboard was broken. He had extra homework to do. And while everyone else had been mean, Rudy had shouted at Frankie and really upset him.

This had been one of the worst days ever.

Rudy let out a deep sigh.
He knew Frankie hadn't meant
to mess everything up.
He was just accident-prone
because he was so big.

And he didn't deserve to be shouted at or have everyone being mean to him.

As bad as today had been for Rudy, he had to admit, Frankie's first day must've been one of the worst in the history of first days.

The chair creaked as Rudy leaned back.

He wished he'd told Mr Hunter what had happened. As much as he didn't like telling tales, everything would've been very different if he had.

Jimmy Voll and the others would be spending their evening doing extra homework, and Rudy might've made a new friend.

But he couldn't change that now.

The best thing he could do was put it right by apologizing to Frankie and helping him settle in.

CHAPTER
FOUR

A short time later, Rudy returned to class, determined to apologize to Frankie.

But Frankie wasn't there.

So Rudy sat down and started making notes for his homework while keeping one eye on the door.

When the bell rang for home time, there was still no sign of him. No boots galumphing down the corridor. No banging and crashing or wreckage of any kind.

He'd totally disappeared!

'I have to find Frankie and apologize,' Rudy told Femi and Edie as they got ready to go.

'I'll say you do!' Edie replied.

'Don't worry, we'll help you,' Femi said.

'Of course, we're a pack.' Edie put her fist into the centre of their huddle.

Rudy and Femi immediately bumped her fist, and they all said, 'For the power of the pack!'

'Yeah! Together we can do anything!' Femi added.

'Thanks, you guys are the best!' Rudy said, and for the first time in hours, he smiled. 'I'll meet you at the Skateway after I've done my homework.'

The afternoon sun was warming the sky as Rudy and his pet wolf cub, Wolfie, arrived at the Skateway. 'How's your Ramp Slam?' Rudy asked Femi.

'I can't get the hang of it,' Femi replied as Wolfie pawed his bandages.

'You will,' Edie said.

'Maybe,' Femi said. 'But it can wait until we've found Frankie.'

'Where do you think he's hiding?' Edie asked.

'I don't know,' Rudy said. 'But there's a way we can find him.'

The wolf boy crouched down and began sniffing the ground. Wolfie joined in too. In a few seconds, Rudy picked up Frankie's scent and they were off!

Street by street, Frankie's trail led them across town. He'd stomped through the park, but he'd ignored the duck pond and hadn't stopped for a go on the swings. He'd skulked through the churchyard and under the railway bridges. But Frankie hadn't checked out the Skateway and he'd ignored all the shops on the High Street, including Carlo's Candy Store, Pluto's Pizzas, and the Slime Fried Chicken Shack. Frankie hadn't

Slime
fried
chicken

even lingered at the window of Flip Kings to check out the new Pitbull-360!

'We're going round in circles,' Femi said as they passed the cinema for the third time. 'My bones are aching!'

'Are you using your noses right?' Edie asked as she crouched down, nose-to-nose with Wolfie.

'Course we are!' Rudy replied.

'So where was Frankie going?' Edie asked.

'I don't know. He must've been lost. He has just moved here,' Rudy said. And with a shrug and a sigh, they set off again.

Despite a few more twists and wrong turns and Wolfie getting distracted by an alley full of bins, Frankie's scent led them down to the dark, forgotten side of town.

Rudy began to suspect where they were heading. But he didn't want to alarm his friends or go there alone.

Away in the distance, thunder rumbled, confirming Rudy's suspicions.

Gradually the sky darkened. But the sun wasn't setting, it was being blotted out by the clouds of a storm that never stops.

The clouds were thick and angry. Thunder rolled and lightning flashed as though they were fighting with genuine hatred.

As they reached the last house in town and turned the corner, the tarmac ran out and all that lay ahead was a dusty dirt track. It looked as though the road builders had refused to go any further.

And who could blame them?

The path only led to one place, up the steep side of a brutal, craggy mountain.

'Who'd want to come here?' Femi asked, nervously gazing up the steep cliff.

'Someone who lives there,' Rudy replied, pointing.

As Edie, Femi, and Wolfie looked up, the thunder crashed and the lightning flashed,

revealing an old abandoned castle, high up on the summit of the craggy rock.

Femi almost jumped out of his bandages. Wolfie let out a whimper. And Edie's ghostly aura dwindled like she was trying to disappear.

'That's High Crag Castle!' Femi wailed. 'We should turn back.'

They'd come a long way, but as Rudy faced up to the dangerous walk that lay ahead, he felt inclined to agree with his friend.

His feet turned, grinding on the gritty path.

'Hey!' Edie said, drifting in front of him. 'You said you wanted to apologize to Frankie. Have you changed your mind?'

'No,' Rudy replied, a little wounded.

'And Frankie's up there?' Edie asked.

Rudy nodded. 'That's where he lives!'

'We can't go there!' Femi gasped. 'You've heard what people say about that place!'

'Yeah, but they're just stories, right?' Rudy said.

Edie looked sheepish.

'This place might look scary, but that doesn't mean it's home to a bunch of monsters,' Rudy continued. 'That's the same mistake Jimmy Voll and everyone at school made about him. He might look like a monster, but he isn't one. He's kind and clever. Even if he is big and clumsy.'

'This place still gives me the creeps,' Femi said as the lightning struck again and Wolfie hid behind him.

'We're a pack, OK?' Edie said, nodding. 'So let's do this!'

'Yeah! We can't let it scare us,' Rudy said. He tipped his head back, took a deep breath, and let out an enormous:

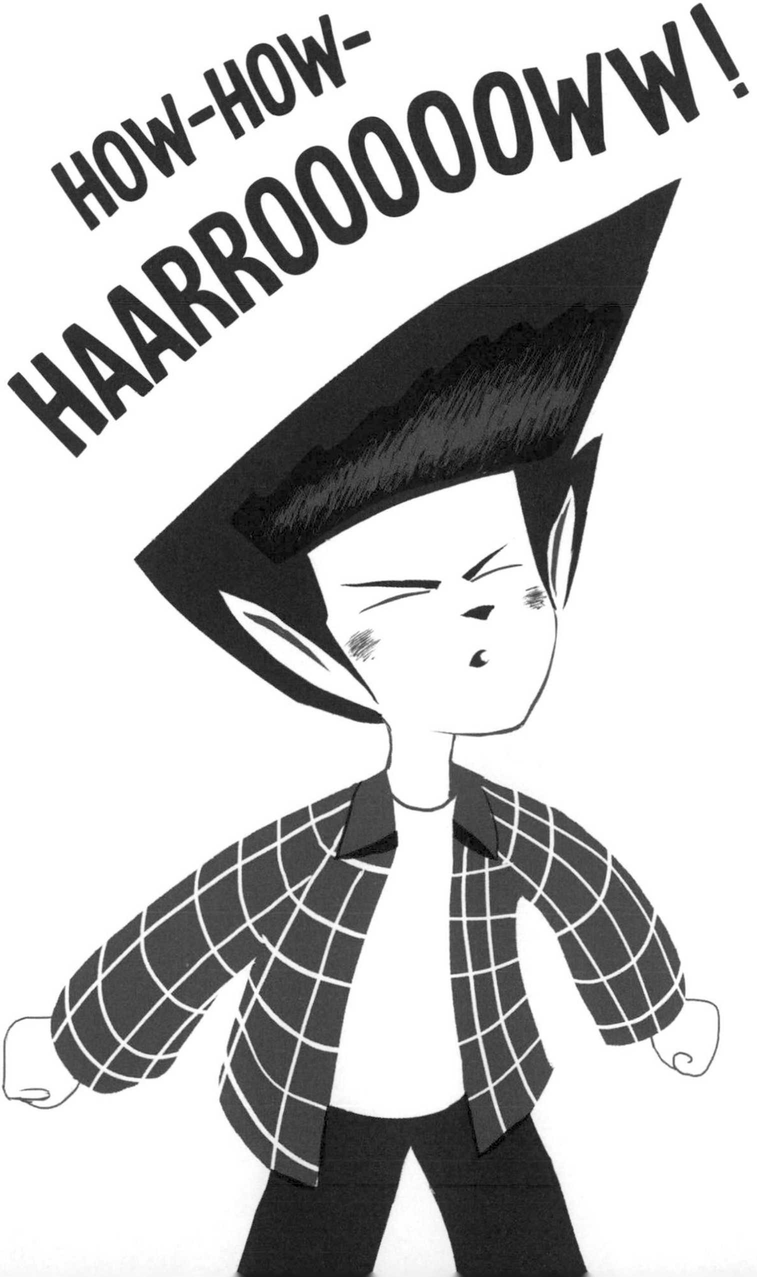
HOW-HOW-
HAARROOOOOOWW!

Rudy's howl gave them all the courage to set off again.

Gradually the narrow winding path led them up between the sharp, jagged rocks jutting from the cliff.

Higher they climbed. The thunder grew louder, and an eerie, pale mist crept in around them.

'I don't like this,' Femi murmured.

'Me neither,' Edie whispered.

'Oh, come—' Rudy began, but he was drowned out by a bone-chilling . . .

YAARRROOOOOO!!

All four of them froze.

Only their eyes dared to move.

'What was that?' Edie whispered.

'I don't know,' Femi replied, his jaw locked like a ventriloquist's. 'Whatever it was, it must've heard your howl!'

'That was no wolf,' Rudy whispered as loud as he dared. 'Or any dog I've ever heard.'

The mist inched in, building a thick wall around them. Wolfie pawed at it, but it only crept in closer.

The gravel on the dirt track crunched as the four of them huddled together.

There was sudden scuffle. Something leaped out of the fog and dived on Rudy, knocking him to the ground—**THUNK!**

Femi pulled his bandages over his eyes and they all screamed:

AAAAAAAAAAAAAHH!

CHAPTER
FIVE

The lightning's raw power lit up the brooding clouds, crackling and sparking as it charged into a thundering—

BOOOOOOMM!

It was so loud, it drowned out Rudy's screams as the big and furry thing pinned him down. Its huge slapping slab of a tongue felt like a slug the size of a beefsteak as it slobbered all over Rudy's face.

'Argh!' Rudy screamed again. But all he got was a mouthful of goo!

He closed his eyes as its taste buds tore at his hair like Velcro, and glistening saliva soaked him like a downpour.

'Pah!' He spat it out.

Rudy opened his blurry eyes. Edie was throwing punches at the beast, but her ghostly fists had no effect! Wolfie was trying to sink his claws in, but they were too short to cut through the beast's fur. Femi had looped a bandage around the beast's collar, but he couldn't rein it in.

Rudy would have to deal with this thing himself.

On the upside, he wasn't actually being eaten. Just licked!

As Rudy tried to push away the slobbering tongue, his fingers tangled in the beast's soggy, lank hair.

URGH!

Sooooo. Much. Slimy. DROOL!

'Get off me!' Rudy yelled, repulsed by the state of himself.

The thing immediately sat up.

Rudy found himself face to face with the snout of what looked like a huge hellhound!

'Is that a dog?' Edie asked.

'Or a bear?' asked Femi.

'I don't know, but it's disgusting!' Rudy said, wiping the drool off his face.

The beast didn't sit like any dogs or bears Rudy had seen. Its back was hunched and its front legs stuck out at angles as if they were different lengths. Or from different animals!

Its tongue lolled out of its mouth like the beast was wearing a tie, which explained why he was sooooo wet!

Wolfie took a
swipe at it, but all he
got was a smattering
of drool!

'It's got a name tag,' Edie said, peering behind the tongue. 'It says: Rocko.'

'Rocko!' Rudy exclaimed. 'He belongs to Frankie.'

'Hey! You said this place wouldn't be home to a bunch of monsters,' Femi said.

'No,' Rudy replied. 'I said we shouldn't assume that!'

'So it could be?' Femi began shaking so violently, his bones rattled.

'It's OK. He's being friendly.' To reassure his friends, Rudy began stroking Rocko. 'Who's a good . . . thing.'

Rocko didn't mind the confusion; he rather liked the attention.

Rudy crouched down. 'Can you find Frankie? Can you, boy? Find Frankie!'

With that, the big bear-like dog bounded off up the path.

'Way to go, Rudy!' Edie put her hand

on her hip. 'Let's follow a crazy monster-dog to a scary old castle in the middle of a thunderstorm.'

'Yeah, this is crazy!' Femi agreed.

'Sorry, but we don't want to get lost,' Rudy said, and they all chased after Rocko.

The mist grew deeper as Rocko panted and clawed his way along the gritty path. Wolfie kept close behind him, sniffing the ground.

'Is this mist?' Edie asked. 'Or Rocko's breath?'

'Trust me, it's mist,' Rudy replied. 'I know what his breath smells like.'

'Ew!' Edie said.

As they rounded a corner, the path opened onto a wide plateau on the clifftop.

'Wow,' Rudy said looking out. 'You can see the whole of Cobble Cross from here.'

'That's not the only thing,' Femi said, and a lightning bolt tore through the clouds. The mist spiralled away as though it was banished and there, looming on the clifftop, was High Crag Castle. It had been abandoned for centuries, until now.

The huge stone blocks in its walls were bound together with ivy. Every window was smashed by the rocky chunks of hail, hurled around by the winter storms.

The roof tiles were chipped and several were missing like aged teeth, and the wind had battered the towers into precarious, twisted ruins.

Only one tower remained, standing defiant and strong against the storm. Its weather-beaten flag was flapping around the pole, trapped in its own private cyclone.

As the lightning fizzled out, the castle was consumed by an icy darkness.

'Oh well, I guess Frankie's out,' Edie said, eyeing the darkened windows.

'Yeah, shame,' Femi added, with phoney disappointment.

But Rudy hadn't come this far to give up so easily.

He strode up to the front door. It was made of solid oak, large and arched. In the centre hung a blackened bronze gargoyle gripping a ring in its teeth.

After his run-in with Rocko, he'd had enough of beasts and their mouths, but there was no doorbell. The thunder rolled like

sticks on a snare as Rudy's trembling hand
reached out and knocked on the door.

He waited, listening, not sure whether anyone inside would've heard him.

'See? He really isn't home,' Femi called out.

Rudy sighed. He felt certain Frankie was here. As he reached out to knock again, the door made a deep—

K-LUNK!

Rudy pulled his hand back as though it was about to be caught in a trap.

The old rusty hinges let out a slow whine. Rudy covered his ears. But it was like a dentist's drill, whistling into his head.

EEEEEEEEEEEAAHH . . .

The door drew open to reveal the slender figure of someone so tall they almost touched the ceiling of the cavernous hallway.

Rudy's eyes opened wide
to take in the sight before
him. Lightning flashed,
illuminating the icy grey
face of a lady with a long
nose that pointed straight at
Rudy. Her eyes burned like
lasers. Towering above her
head was a bushy shock of
jet-black hair, streaked with
two twisting grey spires
that rose like smoke from a
dragon's nostrils.

Rudy realized he
was a long way from the
classroom where he'd felt
fearless. And being here,
facing whoever this was,
made him quake
to his core.

The lady leaned over him and let out a rasping croak.

It wasn't a language Rudy knew. But his parents always told him to be polite. He was about to say 'hello' when the lady convulsed with a spluttering cough—

CA-HUURRR!

A slimy green frog leapt out of her mouth and landed in her hand.

Rudy recoiled in shocked surprise.

'Oh, I'm so terribly sorry,' said the lady, flustered and desperate to hide her embarrassment.

This wasn't what Rudy was expecting.

'I had something in my throat,' she said, quickly composing herself. She dropped the frog and it hopped away.

'It's OK,' Rudy said. His nerves were still rattling, but he found his most polite smile.

'I see you've found Rocko,' she said and called over the big bear-dog.

'Err, yeah,' Rudy said. 'We were actually looking for Frankie. He goes to our school. Is he home?'

The lady smiled. 'I'm afraid he isn't. I haven't seen him since he set off this morning.' Her eyes began searching the swirling mist. 'I do hope he isn't lost. Would you like to come in and have some biscuits while we wait for him?'

'We'd love to—' Rudy said.

'Ooh yes! Biscuits are the best!' Femi added. Edie nodded eagerly, and Wolfie gave a yelp.

'Err sorry,' Rudy said. 'We'd love to, but we really need to see Frankie.'

'Oh, yes,' Femi nodded.

'Well, I'm sorry.' The lady frowned. 'He's not here.'

Rudy stepped back from the door. The wispy mist circled around him and he began to wonder . . .

What's going on here?

Rudy drew a deep sigh, and there, from somewhere in the mist, something made his wolf hackles rise.

As his shoulders hunched and his mind focused, he sniffed, and there it was—

Frankie's scent. And it was fresh!

Rudy's thoughts instantly crystallized. 'He is here!'

The lady's frown deepened.

'Where is he?' Femi asked.

Rudy looked around. He couldn't see past Frankie's mum, but that didn't matter. Frankie's scent couldn't hide!

Forks of lightning shot across the sky like clashing tridents. Deafening thunder erupted, and something rang with a metallic chime.

'He's up there!' Edie cried. 'I saw him!'

Rudy squinted through the clamouring storm. There, on top of the castle, the lightning was striking the flapping flag on top of the bell tower.

'That's it!' Rudy cried. 'Frankie loved watching lightning with his friends!' Rudy turned back to Frankie's mum. 'This may sound a little unusual, but can we go up to your roof?'

To his relief, she smiled. 'Everything is a little unusual here,' she said and welcomed them inside.

CHAPTER SIX

Rudy's trainers pattered against the spiralling stone steps that wound up inside the bell tower. Outside, the storm raged on, hurling rain through the broken windows. The thunder pounded like war drums, and the lightning flashed as though the sky was on fire.

But all Rudy cared about was finding Frankie, and with each step, his scent grew stronger.

Rocko bounded after him. Having one leg shorter than the other made running up the spiral steps easy. And Wolfie, Femi, and Edie kept up, too.

As they approached the top, the clouds
let rip with an almighty thunderclap. The
friends froze, pressing themselves against the
walls like it was an earthquake.

It was enough to make even Rocko quiver.

'Everyone OK?' Rudy asked as the thunder rolled away.

The others nodded and Wolfie gave a yap!

'If this is Frankie's idea of fun, I do not want to see what scares him,' Edie said.

'Come on. We're nearly there,' Rudy said, pointing to a weather-beaten old door that was clinging to its hinges. He pushed it open, and there, sitting huddled on the rain-soaked floorboards was Frankie.

His long arms were hugging his knees to his chest while his flat head rested on his shoulder. As the storm pounded, his eyes gazed up, unblinking and unmoved, lost in a stupor of murky thoughts.

Rocko pushed past Rudy and leapt onto Frankie.

Rudy couldn't tell if it was the smell or the smattering of drool, but either way, the bear-dog made Frankie smile.

As he made a fuss of Rocko, Frankie caught sight of Rudy, Femi, and Edie, standing in the doorway with Wolfie.

'Hello,' he said, surprised.

'Hi,' Rudy said, smiling. The rain-soaked boards squeaked as he stepped closer. 'I came to apologize for shouting at you. I was annoyed because everyone was throwing crystals at us. I was being selfish and I shouldn't have called you a giant disaster. I know you didn't mean to knock over our experiment.'

'I'm just clumsy.' Frankie shrugged. 'Always have been, always will be.'

'I'm also sorry I didn't stick up for you when everyone was whispering in the canteen, and we should've included you in the football. It's made me realize that not being mean isn't enough. You have to stop other people from being mean if you want to make a difference.'

'I'm really sorry, too,' Edie said. 'It was your first day, and we should've helped you, been kinder and better friends. We will be tomorrow, promise.'

'And so will I,' Femi said. 'As long as I'm playing, you'll never feel left out of football or anything else again.'

Wolfie jumped up and gave Frankie a friendly lick.

'Thanks,' Frankie smiled. 'But you don't have to do that. I'm not going back there.'

'Really?' Femi gasped.

'You can't quit after one bad day!' Edie said.

'But I don't fit in,' Frankie replied.

'We'll help you fit in,' Rudy said.

'Oh, look at me,' Frankie said, letting out a sigh.

A flash of lightning lit up Frankie's huge metal boots. His long arms were reaching out of his chequered sleeves while his muscles bulged out through the torn holes. And his kneecaps were bigger than Rudy's shoulders!

'Look at you?' Rudy said. 'Look at us! We don't fit in either, but we fit together— we're a pack. And you can fit with us.'

'That's really kind of you,' Frankie said. 'But what about Jimmy Voll?'

Rudy smiled, flashing his pointy canines.

'Trust me, we can solve that problem, too.'

'Really?' Frankie's eyes opened wide, filling with hope.

'Sure we can.' Rudy smiled.

'All right,' Frankie said and grabbed Rudy in a smothering hug. 'But first, you have to watch the lightning with me. It's amazing!'

As they all settled down to watch the storm, Femi asked: 'Can we have those biscuits now?'

The next morning, Rudy, Femi, and Edie met Frankie outside the school gates. He looked a lot happier today and was walking tall again.

'I got you this to replace the one I broke,' he said and pulled a large Flip Kings bag off his shoulder.

'Wow, thanks!' Rudy said. To his astonishment, inside was a brand new Pitbull-360! 'It's amazing.'

'I'll say!' added Femi.

'Yeah! Too bad we can't hit the Skateway right now,' Edie said.

'Yeah, you could do an awesome Ramp Slam on that!' Femi added.

'It's OK,' Rudy said with a smile. 'There's something we need to do first.

He led the others into the playground where everyone was enjoying a kick about 'Hi. Can we join in?' Rudy called out.

'Not if I've got a say in it!' Jimmy Voll replied, sending a

ripple of sniggering across the playground.

Frankie's shoulders drooped, and he looked like he was about to bolt again.

But Rudy had a plan!

He walked over to Jimmy. 'Hey, you should be nicer to Frankie.'

'Oh yeah? Why?' The devil frowned. Rudy flashed a knowing smile. 'Because he's the best goalie you'll ever get!'

Jimmy's eyes widened as he stared at Frankie. His arms were so long he could reach from post to post, and he was big enough to cover half the net!

'He can stop anything,' Rudy said. 'Even your losing streak!'

Jimmy nodded. 'Yeah, all right. Let's play Three and in!'

Everyone agreed and Frankie stepped into goal. Edie blew her whistle and the game kicked off. Everyone began running around and trying to score three times to take Frankie's place.

But try as they did—*BANG!* Wherever they aimed—*BIFF!* No matter how hard Jimmy kicked it—*BOOF!* Frankie could reach it easily, so no one scored!

Then Rudy passed it
to Femi and—*BANG!* He
hoofed it onto the shed
roof.

'Oh no!' Jimmy cried
as the ball rolled into
the gutter and the game
ground to a halt.

'Sorry,' Femi said,
cringing.

'It's OK,' Rudy said.
'Frankie, can you get it
down, please?'

'Sure,' Frankie replied.

Jimmy and everyone
watched in awe as Frankie
reached up and plucked
the ball out of the gutter.

In less than a minute, they were playing again!

Eventually, the bell rang for morning lessons.

'Frankie, you're amazing! You have to join the school team,' Jimmy gushed as they ran inside.

'Yeah, that'd be great,' Frankie replied.

'See, I knew you'd fit in,' Rudy said, smiling.

'Thanks, Rudy,' Frankie said, and he beamed as he grabbed his new friends in a giant hug.

ABOUT THE
AUTHOR

I write about Rudy and his friends from a
quiet room in my home, tucked away in South
London. To say I love it is an understatement.
It's almost as much fun as actually going on
the adventures with Rudy, or hanging out
with his friends at the Skateway. Although
Rudy is a much better skateboarder than I
am! If you love his stories, give me a

HOW-HOW-HAARROOOOWW!

ABOUT THE
ILLUSTRATOR

George is an illustrator, maker, and avid reader from England. He works digitally and loves illustrating all things curious and mysterious.

FEEL THE POWER OF THE PACK
RUDY
AND THE
WOLF CUB
PAUL
WESTMORELAND
ILLUSTRATED BY
GEORGE ERMOS

TURN THE PAGE
FOR A TASTE OF

RUDY

AND THE

WOLF CUB

CHAPTER ONE

Rudy's skateboard was teetering on the edge of the highest half-pipe in the Skateway. His nerves rattled as he stared down the sheer ramp, which was sloping away like a huge concrete wave.

His two best friends, Femi and Edie, were
watching nearby. Femi was wide-eyed and
waiting to be amazed. Edie's ghostly aura
was glowing with anticipation. But if Rudy
chickened out, they wouldn't think any less of
him.

They all loved practising tricks and
always hung out at the Skateway after school.
But none of them had ever done *The Daring
Double*.

At least, not yet!

'Are you sure about this, Rudy?' Edie called out, as Femi resisted the urge to hide behind his bandages—he couldn't miss this!

The afternoon sun glinted in Rudy's eyes as he gave his friends a reassuring wink. He kicked off. His skateboard hit the ramp. The autumn breeze flicked his spiky fringe, pushing back his little wolf ears.

Rudy's wheels spun in a blur, down the ramp and up the other side, then:

WHOOOSH!

He shot into the air.

Rudy's friends watched, willing him to make it. He grabbed his skateboard and the world spun around him as he flipped in a daring, double somersault.

Femi's and Edie's jaws dropped.

But Rudy landed safely back on his wheels and scraped to a stop at the bottom of the concrete pipe with a pop-slam!

'That was awesome!' Femi cried, almost bursting out of his bandages.

'And ever so slightly . . . *stupid*!' Edie said. 'You are mortal, remember?'

Rudy smiled, flashing his pointy canines. He couldn't believe he'd done it!

'Let me try,' Femi said and ran to the top of the half-pipe.

'Be careful, yeah?' Rudy called out, fearing for his friend.

Femi looked good as he kicked off, but halfway down, a loose bandage caught in his wheels.

Edie and Rudy gasped.

The faster Femi skated, the more his bandages unravelled and tangled until . . .

WHUMP!

Femi's board flipped over and he crash-landed on the ramp, with a ball of bandages round his ankles.

Rudy and Edie ran to their friend. 'Are you OK?' Rudy asked.

Femi groaned and gave them a thumbs-up. Edie clapped her hands, delighted and relieved. 'That was spectacular, Femi. Just not in a good way!'

As she and Rudy began untangling their friend, Rudy froze.

The sound made Rudy's wolf hackles rise. As his mind focused, he dropped everything and shot off across the park, leaving the others staring, open-mouthed.

A moment later, they ran after him.

'What is it?' Femi asked when he and Edie found Rudy crawling around behind the bins.

The answer came as a huge surprise when Rudy emerged holding a little, furry wolf cub.

'*Ahh*, he's adorable,' Femi cooed, as the cub playfully clawed at his loose bandages.

'*Err*, understatement of the year,' Edie said.

'Didn't you hear him whimpering?' Rudy asked.

Femi shook his head. 'We don't have your *insane wolf-hearing*!'

'Or your nose for sniffing out pizza places!' Edie added.

The little cub licked Rudy's nose:

SLURP!

'Where's your pack, little fella?' Rudy asked, stroking the cub's ears.

'Looks like he thinks *you're* his pack,' Femi said as the cub nestled into Rudy's arms.

'Hey.' Edie looked concerned. 'You can't just keep a random wolf cub!' She put her hand on her hip. 'His pack are bound to be looking for him.'

Rudy strained his ears and listened. 'It doesn't sound like it.'

Edie let out an uneasy sigh.

Femi rested his hand on Rudy's shoulder. 'Come on, they must be. Your parents would search the whole town for you.'

'Of course they would,' Edie said. 'A pack will do anything to look after one of its own—working together and helping each other is what packs do!'

'Yeah, you're right,' Rudy said, nodding.

'And that's why he needs his pack,' Femi said. Rudy's eyes lit up.

'He can join mine!'

Femi gulped.

'*Really?*' Edie's eyebrow rose like a question mark. 'You're

just gonna go home and say, *Hey Mum, Dad, I've signed up a new member of the family!'*

'Why not?' Rudy said. 'They'll love him. Wolves are fiercely loyal, you know.'

'Sure,' Edie said, 'but aren't you asking them to be loyal to a *total stranger?'*

Rudy squirmed awkwardly. 'But he's all on his own and needs help. Look at him.'

Femi smiled, stroking the cub. 'He is lovely, but I can't see your parents going for this.'

'Whatever.' Rudy shrugged. He stared into the cub's dark eyes, and the warmth of the little furry bundle seeped through him. He'd only been holding the cub for a minute, but already Rudy couldn't imagine them being apart.

'Come on,' Rudy said. 'Let's go home!'

LOVE RUDY?

WHY NOT TRY THESE TOO . . .